THE CLOCKWORK WAR

By Adam Kline

Illustrations by Dan Whisker

INSIGHT EDITIONS

San Rafael, California

INSIGHT EDITIONS

PO Box 3088
San Rafael, CA 94912
www.insighteditions.com

 Find us on Facebook: www.facebook.com/InsightEditions
Follow us on Twitter: @insighteditions

Library of Congress Cataloging-in-Publication Data available.

ISBN: 978-1-68383-236-2

Publisher: Raoul Goff
Associate Publisher: Jon Goodspeed
Art Director: Chrissy Kwasnik
Senior Designer: Stuart Smith
Managing Editor: Alan Kaplan
Editorial Assistant: Erum Khan
Production Editor: Lauren LePera
Production Manager: Sam Taylor

ROOTS of PEACE REPLANTED PAPER

Insight Editions, in association with Roots of Peace, will plant two trees for each tree
used in the manufacturing of this book. Roots of Peace is an internationally renowned
humanitarian organization dedicated to eradicating land mines worldwide and
converting war-torn lands into productive farms and wildlife habitats. Roots of Peace
will plant two million fruit and nut trees in Afghanistan and provide farmers there
with the skills and support necessary for sustainable land use.

Manufactured in China by Insight Editions

10 9 8 7 6 5 4 3 2 1

for SHK & ELK

CONTENTS

Forewarning

This is not a story about a little girl afraid of kindergarten.

This is a story about pirates, monsters, creepy animatronic dolls, battle, darkness, despair, destruction, and loss. Plus some other things, too. So rest assured that this is most certainly not a story for the faint of heart. On the contrary, it is a story for readers of uncommon taste and courage.

It just happens to begin, very briefly, in the bedroom of a little girl afraid of kindergarten.

CHAPTER I

THE PESSY-MISS

Madeline was frightened. Which was unusual. Madeline was not afraid of snakes, spiders, bedbugs, the bogeyman, or speaking publicly to large groups of people. But today, Madeline was afraid. Thus she had built an impenetrable fortress, constructed of blankets and cushions and guarded by a number of especially faithful stuffed animals, all heavily armed. This fortress, rising from a strategic position high atop her bed, was Madeline's final defense. And her parents could not breach it.

So it was that powerless and desperate, Madeline's parents had retreated downstairs to the kitchen, their base of operations. There, admitting Madeline's terrible power to be greater than their own, they had summoned their most secret and most awesome weapon, which was due to arrive momentarily. This weapon, they agreed, even the mighty Madeline could never resist.

Ding. Dong.

The secret weapon had arrived. And when Madeline's mother opened the door, it smiled with both its heads.

The secret weapon, you see, was Madeline's grand-parents.

The situation was explained. This was a very important day. Quite possibly the most important day in Madeline's life thus far. It was supposed to be fun. It was supposed to be exciting. But Madeline was afraid. And so she had sought refuge in her fortress, where she planned to stay until the very end of time, or at least until it was time for dinner.

"But whatever does she fear?" inquired Madeline's grandmother. "Madeline is normally so very brave!"

"Madeline," whispered Madeline's mother, "is afraid of kindergarten."

The grandmother paused for a moment, then smiled.

"Leave it to me," she said. "I'm a fully licensed grandmother, with considerable experience. And no fortress, however mighty, can stand against me."

"Please hurry," said Madeline's father, a tremor in his voice. "This is her very first day of kindergarten, and class begins promptly at eight."

Madeline's grandmother rolled up her sleeves and climbed the stairs with resolve. Madeline's grandfather, for his part, walked directly to a comfortable leather armchair, sat down with a knowing smile, and immediately fell asleep.

The fortress was a daunting sight, Madeline's grandmother had to admit. She knew at once that sheer force would never win the day. No, she would have to be clever, very clever indeed. So she called for a parley, which is a fancy way of referring to a conversation.

"O Madeline, grim and powerful warlord of this castle, it is I, your grandmother! And I hereby demand a parley!"

There was a pause. Then, very briefly, Madeline's head appeared from between two sheets at the castle gates.

"Hello," said Madeline's head. Then it disappeared, back from whence it came.

"It is my understanding," said the grandmother, choosing her words with care, "that *someone* is afraid of kindergarten."

There was another pause, this one longer than the last. Madeline's grandmother waited patiently. Patience was one of her specialties. Then the head appeared again.

"They'll drop me off at kindergarten," said Madeline, "and I'll be all alone. Without any friends or anything."

"Well," said the grandmother, "it sounds like rather an adventure to me."

"Perhaps," admitted Madeline, "but you see, I am a pessy-miss, which is a little girl who always assumes the worst."

"Ah," said the grandmother. "That's a very big word for such a little girl. I'm quite impressed."

"Thank you," said Madeline, who was remarkably polite, as powerful warlords go.

"But I would imagine," said the grandmother, "that a little girl with such an impressive vocabulary must surely know the true meaning of the word *kindergarten*."

"It is a German word," replied Madeline, "meaning 'children's garden.'"

"That is incorrect," said the grandmother.

"It *is* correct," said Madeline. "I have conducted extensive research."

"Well," smiled the grandmother, "if that is the case, then you certainly have no interest whatsoever in a secret. I thusly declare this parley at an end." And with that, she turned to go.

Madeline paused. A secret was, she considered, rather an intriguing prospect.

"Wait," said Madeline. "I will hear your secret."

Now it was the grandmother's turn to pause. And Madeline wasn't sure if she was going to hear the secret or not. Madeline tried to be patient, but patience wasn't really one of her specialties. So she was very relieved when her grandmother sat down on a little chair by her bed and leaned in close to whisper in her ear.

"*Kindergarten* is a name," whispered the grandmother. "The name of a very special man. Karlheinz Indergarten. Or K. Indergarten. *Kindergarten*, should one omit the punctuation. And it was Mr. K. Indergarten who was responsible for the very first, well, kindergarten. It's named for him, you see."

"I don't believe you," said Madeline, who had conducted extensive research.

"We have established that you are a pessy-miss," replied the grandmother. "Now shall I continue or not?"

"Yes," said Madeline. "But please understand that I have certain reservations."

"Oh, my dear Madeline," smiled the grandmother, "everyone has reservations about kindergarten—at first."

CHAPTER 2

THE SECRET OF KINDERGARTEN

It was in the old country, in a little village by the sea, where horses' hooves clippety-clopped along the most magnificent cobblestone streets.

The smell of fresh muffins was always in the air, and twinkly eyed old men held court outside the pub, clinking their glasses and smiling at everyone. Everywhere you'd turn, there was a big, slobbery dog with a stick just right for throwing. And in the midst of it all was Miss Understood's Preparatory School and Home for Orphaned Children, which was a modest sort of school, but cheerful and cozy all the same.

This is where the village children came to learn, and this is where some of them lived. All of them very much liked their teacher, a kind and gentle woman named Miss Understood. But while Miss Understood was certainly very wise, sometimes she would say things that didn't seem quite right.

When it was time to wake the children, for instance, she'd say, "Wake up, children, wake up! The early nerd gets the worm!" Which isn't quite right, as you know. But everyone knew what she meant, most of the time, even though she was Miss Understood.

Now in all the village, and for miles and miles well beyond that, one marvel surpassed all others—even the muffins. That was the tree: great, great grandfather to every ancient oak as far as the eye could see, and farther. Its trunk was as thick as twenty fat men, and it had been that way as long as anyone could remember.

Older folks would nap in its shade, and even the most courageous of men found a certain reassurance in its strength. But the children loved it best, and with good reason. For the lowest branches formed a sort of stair, positively irresistible to anyone who liked to climb trees. And because the tree was conveniently located at the very center of a park, at the very center of town, directly across the street from Miss Understood's school, this stair saw a great deal of traffic indeed. Everyone loved the tree.

But among all the village children, there were none who loved the tree more than Karlheinz Indergarten and Leopold Croak. The two were the closest of friends, and in the devoted care of Miss Understood. For both had lost their moms and dads. But when the sun shone on their mighty tree, they hadn't a care in the world. For while there were many things the children didn't have, what they did have was the greatest thing of all. And that was imagination.

Karlheinz and Leopold would imagine that the tree was a castle. Sometimes it was a mountain, covered in ten feet of snow. It was even a giant who would pick the children up, put them on his shoulders, and tell them stories. The tree, you see, was whatever they imagined it to be. Imagination is a kind of magic.

On this particular afternoon, Miss Understood turned to Karl, and to Leopold, and asked, "So children, what is your tree today?"

And Leopold, who had a very fine imagination, cried out, "A pirate ship!"

Karl watched as the tree changed. Before he could even blink, it was a tree no more. There, floating proudly on an endless ocean of azure blue, was a pirate ship. As Miss Understood stood watching, the two friends ran forward and climbed aboard. Every pirate ship, after all, requires pirates.

"Avast, me hearties!" yelled Karl. "Slack off the main-sheet! Let over the jib and take in the boom-tackles! Coil the halyards and gasket the foresail!"

But the pirate Leopold just stood there. He didn't coil or gasket anything. He simply raised a stick, which transformed into a sword. And when he spoke, there was challenge in his voice.

"I'll do no such thing, Cap'n, until you've found your manners."

Captain Karl didn't like the sound of that at all. So he replied in a menacing tone, "Obey, ye scurvy dog, or you'll have no grog tonight!"

"We ain't seen land for weeks," said Leopold, "nor gold nor silver neither! And there's murmurs and rumblings that you ain't fit to lead this dreadful pirate ship!"

"Impudent wretch!" bellowed Karl. "Why, I'll lash ye to the mizzenmast and tan your mutinous hide!"

"Me and the crew thinks otherwise, Cap'n," said Leopold, raising an eyebrow.

"What crew?" demanded Karl, who didn't see a crew of any kind except for his friend.

Then on the deck behind Leopold appeared a crew of fearsome pirates, with eye patches and beards and swords that flashed in the sun. The boys' imaginations were really good ones.

Captain Karl could see that Leopold and his mutinous cohorts were up to no good. And if he didn't do something drastic, he might not be captain much longer, which seemed to Karl an unthinkable circumstance altogether. So he raised his own stick, which fast became a sword, and cried out, "Motherless devils! To the death!"

With that he clutched a rope, swung down upon them, and attacked.

The battle was terribly exciting. Captain Karl was hopelessly outnumbered, but he was remarkably brave. As he swung his sword, he cast the pirates overboard in droves. None could resist him, and even the bilge rats scurried to hide as Karl clomped toward Leopold in his big black boots. Leopold, you see, was the leader of the mutiny, and the boys would have to have a duel.

But even as their swords clashed, Miss Understood stood at the edge of the park and watched as a storm rolled in. This was a real storm, from the real ocean, and the sky grew terribly dark. Miss Understood watched the real storm, then turned to the boys playing in the tree, and realized they were in real danger.

"Come in, children, come in!" she cried. "Teleport in a storm!"

But Karl and Leopold were far too busy playing. To them, Miss Understood's cries of concern weren't really anything to be concerned about.

"Do ye hear the sirens' cries?" yelled Karl. "They call for thy doom!" With that, he swung his sword yet again and drove Leopold onto the plank, which is what pirates have to walk when they've been naughty.

Leopold tried and tried to fight back, but Captain Karl was too fierce.

"Now yield, brazen scum!" yelled Karl. "Or face the terrors of the deep!"

Standing at the end of the plank and trying not to fall, Leopold looked down. There were sharks swimming in the water, and they looked hungry for something other than muffins. So he lowered his sword and sighed.

"Captain Karlheinz," he said, "you have defeated me with your superior swordplay. I hereby swear allegiance to thee and thee alone, forever and ever, until the end of time—or at least until it's time for dinner. I'm sorry for leading a mutiny against you."

"Apology accepted," smiled Karl, lowering his sword. With that, the sword was once again a stick, and the ship was once again a tree. The sharks all disappeared, and beneath Leopold's feet was not the dreaded plank, but a tree branch.

Karl and Leopold smiled at each other. Pretending to be pirates had been really fun. They were lucky to have such fine imaginations.

"That was great!" said Karl.

"Aye aye, Cap'n," said Leopold. "One of our best adventures yet."

That's when a very real bolt of lightning hit Leopold Croak, from the very real storm now raging above the tree, and knocked him to the ground far below. Miss Understood rushed to his side and scooped him up in her arms. And Karl's face grew wet, but not entirely from rain.

CHAPTER 3

QUITE INCURABLE

Dr. Pimpledink bustled about his examining room, poking and prodding Leopold. He took the boy's temperature and tested his reflexes. He massaged his two temples, and then his solar plexus. He stared down his throat. He tickled his toes. He checked the boy's pulse, then looked up his nose. And all the while, Karlheinz and Miss Understood stared at Leopold with grave concern while Leopold stared back and said nothing.

Finally, after a great deal of mumbling and fumbling

about, Dr. Pimpledink sat back, adjusted his spectacles, and declared Leopold fit as a fiddle and healthy as a horse.

But Miss Understood was not so sure. Miss Understood knew about such things. When she looked into the boy's eyes, she thought that Leopold did not seem quite like Leopold.

"He looks different," whispered Miss Understood. "He looks . . . older, somehow."

Dr. Pimpledink followed Miss Understood's gaze and stared into Leopold's eyes.

"Hmm," said Dr. Pimpledink. "Perhaps . . . a final test. Half a moment!"

Dr. Pimpledink rustled around in a dusty drawer, mumbling to himself all the while, and Karl gazed at his friend. Yes, thought Karl, something is different. Something is wrong.

"Aha!" said Dr. Pimpledink, producing a thick stack of papers. "Now then, young man, tell me what you see!"

On the first sheet of paper was an inkblot, though to Karl it looked like something more than that.

"An inkblot," said Leopold.

"Mm hmm," said Dr. Pimpledink. "And this one?"

"An inkblot," said Leopold again.

"I see," said Dr. Pimpledink, his eyes narrowing with concern. "And this one?"

"An inkblot," said Leopold, shrugging his shoulders. They all looked the same.

Dr. Pimpledink frowned, then rose and waddled to his desk. There he paged quickly through a great big book, scanning the pages and mumbling to himself. At length, he shut the book, glanced once more at Leopold, and took Miss Understood by the arm, drawing her into the hall. When he spoke, he tried to be very quiet. But Karl could both see and hear him through a small crack in the office door.

"I'm afraid this is rather grave," said the doctor. "It appears that . . . well, you see, it appears this little boy has lost his imagination."

"But you will fix him," replied Miss Understood. "You will fix him at once!"

Dr. Pimpledink wrung his hands a bit, then removed his spectacles. He didn't want to tell Miss Understood the truth, because it was unpleasant. But Miss Understood stood waiting with a stern look in her eye, and the doctor knew he had no choice.

"It's impossible to fix a broken imagination,"

whispered Dr. Pimpledink. "The condition is quite incurable, I'm afraid."

———•———

The following day, Leopold rose from his bed, right next to Karl's, in a cozy room just above Miss Understood's kitchen. And as all the other children yawned and stretched, Karl watched him.

He didn't yawn. He didn't stretch. He didn't smile. He simply buttoned his shirt, zipped his fly, and walked downstairs.

As the other children ate their porridge, they giggled and wriggled in their seats. But Leopold didn't giggle or wriggle, the way he usually did. He simply ate his porridge, right down to the very last morsel, and walked outside. As Karl followed, watching his friend, Miss Understood followed as well, watching Karl.

Leopold stood all by himself, staring across the street at the tree. Miss Understood watched as Karl slowly approached his friend and spoke.

"Hello," said Karl.

"Hello," said Leopold.

"I . . . I was thinking of our tree during the night,

and of today's adventure," said Karl. "I thought perhaps today, our tree might be a bank, in the Wild American West. I could be an outlaw, and try to rob the bank, and you could be a sheriff, and send me off to jail. Of course, there would have to be a great deal of dramatic gunplay prior to my inevitable defeat."

Leopold paused and considered. Karl waited, with bated breath, to see what he would say. So did Miss Understood.

"But," said Leopold at length, "it's only a tree."

Only then did Karl know, beyond doubt, that his very best friend had lost his imagination. It made him want to cry.

"Miss Understood," inquired Leopold, "may I practice my arithmetic?"

Miss Understood could only nod, and stare at little Karl as his friend walked briskly away. Miss Understood wanted to cry as well.

That night, Karl sat at his desk in Miss Understood's humble classroom. Miss Understood sat nearby and wondered if she was doing the proper thing. She had been doing a great deal of thinking, you see, and had finally decided that there was nothing she could do to help Leopold, given that a broken imagination is impossible to fix.

But perhaps there was something she could do for Karl. So she had sent for an old acquaintance, with a message to come posthaste. Teacher and student had been waiting ever since, and now it was late at night— almost bedtime.

Then came a knock at the door, and in walked a very old man, who was a clockmaker.

"Karl," said Miss Understood, "I have someone I'd like you to meet."

The old man walked forward and knelt by Karl's desk. Karl found it strange that the old man kept his hands in his pockets, but he didn't really care. He was too busy thinking about Leopold.

"Karl," said the clockmaker, "I wonder if I might see your hands. You know, you can tell a great deal about someone by looking at their hands."

Karl put his hands on his desk, where a single shaft of moonlight shone brightly down upon them.

"Ah," smiled the clockmaker, "slender fingers. This is good. And very clean. These are good hands, very good. These are hands a boy should be proud of."

Karl looked at his hands. He hadn't really noticed them before.

"I am a great expert on hands," whispered the clockmaker. "And perhaps you wonder why."

Karl didn't know what to say, so he said nothing. The clockmaker took his own hands from his pockets and showed them to Karl.

"Because mine no longer work."

The clockmaker's hands were gnarled, and the fingers didn't move the way they should. They were old hands, and using them had become painful for the clockmaker. This sometimes happens when hands get very old. Karl was sad for the clockmaker, but the clockmaker wasn't sad. He knew that his hands were like clocks, and sometimes old clocks just don't work as well as new ones. It wasn't something to cry about. It was simply the way things were.

Karl looked from the clockmaker's hands to his bright and twinkly eyes, and he could see that the clockmaker was a man who understood things.

"I've lost my best friend," said Karl.

"It isn't easy to be without a friend," said the clockmaker. "Perhaps what you need . . . is a new one."

The clockmaker extended his hand in friendship.

Karl paused just briefly, and took it. The hand was warm. It was still a good hand, thought Karl, even if it didn't work precisely right.

Moments later, Miss Understood waved and waved from beneath the mighty oak as Karl and the clockmaker strode into the night. Miss Understood felt both very happy and very sad all at once, which is a curious way to feel. But when Karl and the clockmaker had finally faded away and melted into the shadows, Miss Understood allowed herself a single tear. She then spoke softly to the tree, and for some reason, this time, she spoke her words just right.

"Time heals all wounds."

CHAPTER 4

THE LITTLE THINGS

Karl and the clockmaker had walked very, very far—much farther than Karl had ever walked before. Karl was to be the clockmaker's apprentice, and learn the art of clockmaking, and live with the clockmaker in his workshop. The workshop sat on a hill, which overlooked a meadow, and there was a gravel path leading to its door. The gravel made crunchy sounds when Karl walked on it. It was a sound he liked.

Now Karl sat on a stool in the workshop and listened to the clocks. There were clocks everywhere: big clocks, little clocks, cuckoo clocks, and grandfather clocks, as well as many others. And they all made the same magical sound.

Tick. Tock. Tick. Tock.

Karl liked this sound as well. As he listened to the ticks and the tocks, he watched the great big pendulum of a great big clock as it slowly swung back and forth, like a trapeze artist who had fallen asleep on his trapeze.

When the clockmaker sat down on his own stool, he noticed Karl's interest straight away. Big clocks are always very impressive to people who don't yet know about clocks.

"A most impressive chronometer," said the clock-maker. "Very big, for very important people. Very important people always think bigger is better. 'Time is money! Time is money! Look, everyone! Look at me! Look how important I am!' That's what very important people always say."

The clockmaker paused, and they listened to the ticking of the clocks.

"But time is not money," whispered the clock-maker. "Time is magic."

The clockmaker opened a drawer in his workbench, and with it, the door to a tiny, magical world.

The drawer was filled with watches, the kind
one has to wind to make work. Most of the watches
weren't quite finished, but all of them had been freshly
wound. As Karl looked and listened, all the little gears
and cogs spun and hummed and ticked and tocked,
like a million tiny fairies hard at work. It was the most
wonderful thing he had ever seen.

"Bigger is seldom better," whispered the clockmaker.
"It's the little things that have the most potential."

With that, the clockmaker slid a small brown paper
package across the bench to Karl. The package was tied
with string, and the clockmaker smiled to himself as
Karl unwrapped it.

Inside was a little leather case. On its shell,
engraved in the leather, it read "K. Indergarten." That
was Karl's name. The clockmaker smiled again as Karl
opened the case to find a tiny set of tools, tiny tools for
handling tiny gears and cogs. These would be Karl's
tools, with which he would become a clockmaker.

Karl had never gotten a present before. And even
though he still felt sad about Leopold, it was difficult not to smile. So Karl smiled, and the clockmaker
smiled back. Neither one of them had smiled much
recently, so they enjoyed it very much.

Dingalingaling!

That was the sound of someone at the front counter. The clockmaker rose from his stool and walked from the back of the workshop to the front. There at the counter was an especially fancy sort of customer, holding an especially fancy sort of clock.

"Mrs. Goodnight!" said the clockmaker. "Good morning!"

"Is it?" inquired Mrs. Goodnight.

"Good?" asked the clockmaker.

"Morning."

"It is indeed," said the clockmaker.

"I wouldn't know," said Mrs. Goodnight.

"This is something we shall have to remedy!"

"Such is my hope," said Mrs. Goodnight. "Sir Percy insists upon a highball at precisely five o'clock."

"Ah," said the clockmaker. "And your clock is not precise!"

"Precisely."

"Then it's time I got to work!" said the clockmaker.

"Good day," said Mrs. Goodnight.

"Good day, Mrs. Goodnight. Good day."

As Mrs. Goodnight crunch-crunched away back down the gravel path, the clockmaker stared at the clock. It was a very expensive clock, with a great many shiny little parts. It would be a very complicated repair, the clockmaker knew. It would probably take a very long time. He had better get to work straight away! So the clockmaker picked up the clock, with his hands that didn't work quite right, and turned to walk to his workbench.

Then his hands, which used to work so well, dropped the clock. And to the clockmaker, time seemed to stop as it fell.

The clock shattered, and the clockmaker's heart shattered with it. The clockmaker watched in horror as thousands of tiny gears and cogs rolled across the floor, all in different directions. One tiny cog rolled slowly away, away from its brothers and sisters, and finally came to rest against Karl's foot.

The clockmaker stared at Karl. Karl stared at the clockmaker. Neither knew quite what to say. The clockmaker stared at Karl, and then at his hands, which had betrayed him. And bowing his head, sad and defeated, the clockmaker slowly turned away and walked upstairs. There was nothing to say and nothing to do, so the clockmaker had decided to go to sleep, in hopes that he would dream of better times.

As the clockmaker closed his eyes, Karl picked up the tiny cog that had come to rest against his foot. It seemed to Karl that the cog had come to him for a reason. And Karl's eyes were open, more open than they had ever been before.

The next morning, the clockmaker awoke to an unfamiliar sound.

"I don't know that chime," said the clockmaker. With that, he arose from his bed and slowly walked downstairs.

Karl was seated at the workbench. Before him sat the clock.

Tick. Tock. Tick. Tock. These are the sounds that came from the clock.

When the clockmaker had gone to bed, the clock's tiny gears and cogs had been scattered across the floor. But now they were all working together, just right. The clockmaker didn't quite know what to make of that. Karl turned to him and smiled.

"You have done this?" asked the clockmaker.

Karl nodded. He had worked all night to help the clockmaker and the clock.

"And how exactly?" demanded the clockmaker. "Tell me at once!"

"I had to take apart some other clocks first, to see how they worked," said Karl.

"Which clocks?"

Karl pointed to a number of clocks on the wall.

"This one, and this one, and this one, and these."

The clockmaker stood still for a moment, aghast. His mouth was slightly open, as if he wanted to say something. But he didn't know quite what to say. So instead of saying something, the clockmaker walked slowly to the workbench. Opening a secret drawer, he withdrew a small wooden box, which he placed before Karl.

"Open it," said the clockmaker.

Karl opened the box. Inside was the most magnificent pocket watch in the whole world. It was a beautiful thing that made beautiful sounds, and to Karl, the sounds weren't like the sounds from other clocks. The sounds were like a song. It was as if the pocket watch were singing, just for Karl.

"It is my masterpiece," whispered the clock-maker.

"It's perfect," whispered Karl.

"Nothing is perfect," said the clockmaker. "But it is very close."

"It's wonderful," said Karl. "It's the most wonderful thing imaginable."

"No, Karl," said the clockmaker. "You are."

⸺⸺⸺⸺⸺⸺

Several years passed. Karl was a little older, and so was the clockmaker. The clockmaker walked more slowly, and he slept a little longer every night. But the clockmaker was very happy. Because he knew that each morning, when he entered the workshop to start the day, Karl would surprise him yet again.

The clockmaker entered the workshop, and when Karl held out his hand, the clockmaker gasped.

Sitting on Karl's hand was a clockwork butterfly. And even as the clockmaker watched, the butterfly stretched its wings and rose into the air.

The butterfly flew twice around the clockmaker's head, and the clockmaker felt as if his heart were flying with it. Then it landed on his shoulder, very close to the clockmaker's ear. He could hear the whir of little gears and cogs. But even though the butterfly had landed, the clockmaker's heart continued to fly.

"She is wondrous, Karl," said the clockmaker. "She is astonishing. She is beautiful beyond compare."

Karl smiled. He liked the butterfly, too.

"You know," said the clockmaker, "a boy with such a gift as yours could be a very important person, if he wanted."

"No," said Karl. "I don't think I'd like that much at all. I just like to make things."

"Good," replied the clockmaker. "Very good. This is just what a true artist should say."

Several more years passed. Karl got a little older, and the clockmaker got very old indeed. Now his hands barely worked at all, and Karl had to help him cut his food. But the clockmaker had never been happier. It never occurred to him that with every passing day, he grew older. Because with every passing day, he grew more proud. Karl made him feel so proud that he never thought about much else.

When the clockmaker entered the workshop and sat down upon his stool, Karl placed a little metal box before him. As the clockmaker watched, the box slowly opened, all on its own.

Inside was a nest. In it were five little eggs, made of metal. Before the clockmaker could utter a word, the eggs began to quiver. And then they hatched, revealing five tiny clockwork robins, who opened their eyes and sang a song.

Tenderloin, truffles, and goose pâté,
Caviar and crème brûlée,
Thank you, no, but don't be hurt,
Just bring us a fresh patch of dirt.
Worms, marvelous worms!
Squiggly and wriggly and squirming!
Worms, marvelous worms!
Their meat is the treat that we're yearning!

"Why," said the clockmaker, "I believe they want their breakfast!"

Karl smiled and opened a drawer at the back of the box. From this drawer he withdrew five wriggling clockwork worms and carefully fed them to the robins. The robins enjoyed their breakfast very much. In fact, they enjoyed it so much that when they finished, they decided to sing all over again. Chirp, chirp, chirp!

"It is the most magnificent thing I have ever seen," said the clockmaker. "It is perfect."

"Nothing is perfect," said Karl. "But it is very close."

Years passed. Karl was no longer a boy, but a young man. He was, perhaps, a little thin, as young men go. And he was, perhaps, a little shy, at least around people other than the clockmaker. The clockmaker had become Karl's best friend. His only other friends were things he made.

When the clockmaker entered the workshop, Karl thought that he had never seen a man so old. He walked so slowly that he scarcely seemed to be moving at all. But Karl waited very patiently, and at long last the clockmaker arrived at his stool to see what Karl had made. Though the twinkle in his eye was not as bright as it had been when first they met, it had not yet been extinguished.

The clockmaker looked at Karl, and Karl looked at the clockmaker. The clockmaker waited.

Then there was a movement in the pocket of Karl's shirt.

From the top of the pocket peeked a little clock-work mouse. The mouse looked at the clockmaker, and its whiskers twitched as it smiled. The clockmaker smiled back, and the twinkle in his eye grew brighter than ever before.

The mouse climbed from Karl's pocket and scurried down his arm to the workbench. Once on solid ground, the mouse began to dance. The mouse was a very good dancer, and the clockmaker clapped his hands with joy.

The mouse bowed with tremendous formality, in thanks for the applause. He was a very polite little mouse.

"His name is Pim," whispered Karl.

The clockmaker rose very slowly and kissed Karl's forehead, the way a father sometimes kisses his son.

"Magical, Karl," said the clockmaker. "A magical little mouse. But now . . . you must excuse me. I'm feeling rather . . . unwound."

The clockmaker slowly turned, and Karl watched as he slowly made his way back to bed. As the clockmaker was falling asleep, he thought about the butterfly, and the robins, and Pim. He was very proud. And as the clockmaker's thoughts turned to Karl, his heart stretched its wings and flew away.

One week later, Karl sat at the workbench, listening to the clocks.

Tick. Tock. Tick. Tock.

The clockmaker's stool was empty.

Pim stared at Karl, unsure of what to do. Pim thought briefly that he might dance for Karl, in hopes of making him feel better. But that didn't seem quite right. So instead, Pim simply sat and waited, his whiskers twitching slightly as he watched the man who had made him.

Then the clocks struck noon, all at once, and their chimes all rang twelve times.

Dong. Dong. Dong. The chimes were very loud, and it seemed to Karl that they were saying something.

His time here had come to an end.

As the last great "dong" echoed slowly into silence, Karl rose from his stool.

"Pim," he said, "it's time to go home."

CHAPTER 5

MONEY CAN FRY HAPPINESS

The very next morning, Karl strode through the countryside, walking a path he hadn't walked in many years. He carried only a small satchel, his case of tiny tools, and Pim, who peeked from Karl's shirt pocket. He walked very fast, now that his mind was made up.

Karl thought it strange that as they neared the village, the sky grew darker. It was only late morning after all.

But at the outskirts of the village, Karl found that it had changed. A thick black smog hovered in the air, and great towers sprouted gigantic from the center of town. Some of these towers had enormous chimneys at the top, which belched soot and, in some cases, flame.

Pim didn't like the look of this at all. But Karl strode forward into the blackness, and if he was afraid, he didn't show it.

What Karl found he scarcely recognized.

The bakeries had all disappeared, and the pub was all boarded up. Where horses had once clippety-clopped down glistening cobblestone streets, now there was only black muck. And while Karl recalled a great many big, slobbery dogs who always liked to play fetch, the dog who limped toward him now looked only hungry.

Karl could tell that it had once been a very good dog. But something bad had happened, and now the dog didn't trust people the way it had in the past. So Karl reached into his satchel and broke his sandwich in two. Half of it he offered to the dog.

The dog paused, as if uncertain of Karl's intent. Then, quick as can be, it lunged forward to snatch the sandwich in its jaws and quickly wolf it down. Karl felt lucky that he had not been bitten.

Pim, who was a very polite little mouse, thought the dog had shown very poor manners indeed. So he scolded the dog quite hotly, and shook his little fist in warning. "You'd better be nice, or else!" he seemed to say.

The dog gave Pim a sheepish, guilty look. He knew that he had been bad. He had just been so very hungry. The dog slunk off into an alley and felt terrible about the whole affair. Perhaps one day, when he was not so hungry, he would show the little mouse what a good dog he truly was.

But Pim had other things to think about, for Karl was walking fast again, headed straight for the center of town. When he got there, he caught his breath and held it, then sighed a long, sad sigh.

Miss Understood's Preparatory School and Home for Orphaned Children had always been a humble sort of place, but now it was falling apart. The gutters sagged, and the roof was missing most of its shingles. Several windows were broken, and the front door hung at a funny angle. And everywhere, all around the school, towered big, dark buildings that frowned down from high above.

Then Karl turned to spy his tree, the mighty oak, which was dying.

Cloaked in the shadow of the towers and covered in layers of soot, the tree could no longer grow. Instead, it had begun to slowly shrink, as if it were retreating. When Karl was a boy, he used to think that the tree had so many leaves, it would take him a hundred years to count them all. Now Karl could count the leaves quite easily. There were three.

"My dear Karlheinz," said a voice, "you have returned to me."

There, coming forward from shadow, was Miss Understood, and she reminded Karl of the tree.

Her hair had turned iron gray, and she walked hunched slightly over, as if carrying some great invisible burden. Her dress was covered in patchwork, and her shoes were stuffed with paper to cover the holes in their soles. And yet upon seeing Karl, she smiled. She was still Miss Understood after all, and Karl knew that her spirit was still strong.

"I'm so glad you're home," said Miss Understood.

"Everything is dead," said Karl, "or dying."

"Yes, it is hard for things to grow here now," sighed Miss Understood. "So much darkness, and filth. This is not good for trees, you know . . . or for children."

Karl thought of the children. The village must be a scary place for them, he thought.

"But!" said Miss Understood. "There are good

things, too! Our town is very rich, and everyone has heard of us, because of Emma Cuddles!"

"Emma Cuddles?" said Karl. "Who is Emma Cuddles?"

"She is our ambassador to the world," said Miss Understood. "And she is very popular in America. She is a doll, Karl, and she is quite remarkable. You see, Emma Cuddles is made to love the children. Whenever a little boy or girl is near, Emma Cuddles hugs them."

"Do the children like to be hugged by Emma Cuddles?" asked Karl.

"I suppose so," said Miss Understood. "But I am very lucky, you know. I have many children to hug. And my hugs are real, because I feel them in my heart. But this Emma Cuddles . . . I don't think she has a heart."

Just then, a little girl went running by, chased by a doll.

"HUG ME, HUG ME, HUG ME!" cried the doll.

But the little girl didn't want to be hugged by Emma Cuddles. The little girl didn't like Emma Cuddles at all.

Sometimes toys seem wonderful to parents, you see, but not to children. This was the case with Emma

Cuddles. Parents everywhere, all over the world, thought Emma Cuddles was cute. But children found her frightening. Oddly enough, people often buy deeply flawed products, sometimes in vast quantities, thanks to a phenomenon known as "advertising."

Karl watched as the girl ran away, chased by Emma Cuddles. He thought the doll seemed awful. Karl knew things most adults don't know.

"What a horrid little doll," said Karl.

"Perhaps," said Miss Understood. "But she has made him very rich."

"Exactly whom has she made rich?" inquired Karl.

"Why," said Miss Understood, "our Leopold of course!"

Karl turned to gaze at the nearest great building. On its side were the words "Cuddlecom Incorporated," and in one big window, directly at its center, stood Leopold Croak, staring down at them.

He had once been Karl's best friend. But now he didn't look so friendly.

"He is a very important person," said Miss Understood. "Very good with numbers. And he is the richest man in the world. But alas, money can fry happiness."

CHAPTER 6

THE SPIDER AND THE FLY

The next morning, as everyone in the village went to work at Leopold's factories, they noticed something different. One small shop, which had been boarded up the day before and covered in dirt and grime, had been cleaned. The boards had been removed, and painted on the front window, in big gold letters, were the words "K. Indergarten Clock & Watch Repair."

The store looked very pretty, and it made the villagers feel good somehow. But this feeling quickly passed when they went to work in the factories.

Karl worked all morning, cleaning his little shop. But when it came time to have lunch, he locked the door and went to the park, with a sandwich and a great big book, which he had decided to read.

Karl sat in the park and ate his sandwich and opened his great big book. Then he had a curious feeling, and looked up.

All around the park, hiding in shadows, were children. They looked as if they were waiting for something to happen.

Then, high above, the sun appeared from behind a tower as it made its way across the sky. As the sun shone down, a few bright beams of golden sunshine reached the tree. And as they did, the children all ran forward to play in its black limbs.

The children all seemed happy, and Karl thought for just a moment that the tree seemed happy, too.

But the sun quickly disappeared behind another tower, and the park was bathed in darkness yet again. The children all climbed down and walked away, looking very sad. Karl thought the tree looked sad as well, and as he watched, a single leaf fell from the tree and floated slowly to the ground.

Karl looked up at the tower that the sun had

slipped behind. It was the tallest tower of them all, and at its very top was a window. In the window stood a little girl whose name was Agatha. Agatha stared at Karl, and Karl waved to her. But Agatha quickly shut the drapes and disappeared.

"And whaddya got for me today, insect?" came a voice.

Karl turned to see a man holding a boy by his ear. The man was being mean, because he was a bully. And the boy, whose name was Toby, was afraid of him.

"Nothing!" cried Toby. "I swear!"

The man picked up Toby and shook him very hard. As Toby shook, Karl could hear the distinctive jingle of coins.

"Nothin' don't jingle," said the bully.

"I earned it!" squealed Toby. "I pulled weeds for a lady!"

"Now I know you're lying," said the bully. "Weeds don't grow here. Nothin' does."

"You don't know everything!" cried Toby.

The bully turned Toby upside down, shook the coins from his pockets, and picked them up.

"Well, I do know this," said the bully. "*Now* you've got nothin'."

The bully strode off, laughing to himself, as Toby ran away. Karl thought he had never seen such an awful thing, except for maybe Emma Cuddles. And though the bully was a very big bully with great big muscles, Karl followed him down a dark and narrow alley.

The bully was laughing and counting the money he had stolen. But even as he did, he walked straight into a spider web. And the spider, which was very surprised, scuttled across his forehead in dismay.

The bully screamed so loud that Karl had to cover his ears. And as the bully sprinted away, screaming in terror, Karl knew something he never would have guessed.

The bully was afraid of spiders.

So Karl strode for his shop, his book clutched under his arm, thinking about bullies and spiders. He would have to weave a web of his own.

When Toby awoke the next morning, he yawned and stretched his arms. He was thirsty. But when he reached for his glass of water, which Miss Understood always left on his bedside table, he found an unexpected thing.

It was a package, wrapped neatly in brown paper.

And tied to the package, with a little bit of string, was a small card, which Toby picked up and read.

With Kind Regards from K. Indergarten

That's what the little card said.

Toby didn't quite know what to make of that. And so he opened the package.

Inside the package was a small vest, just his size, made of metal. It was very shiny, and Toby thought he had never seen anything more beautiful. Then he noticed a little button on the vest, which said "PRESS HERE."

Toby didn't quite know what to make of that, either.

◦———————•

Toby walked through the village. He was hoping to pull some more weeds and earn a little money. If he hurried, maybe he could pull a great many weeds, and the lady would give him a biscuit for a treat. That sounded very fine to Toby, and so he took a shortcut, down a dark and narrow alley.

But Toby soon regretted his decision, when he bumped straight into the kneecaps of the bully.

"Alright, insect," grinned the bully. "Let's have it."

"Leave me alone!" cried Toby. "You're a big, wicked brute, and I don't like you one bit!"

The bully didn't care if Toby liked him or not. So he snatched him up with both big arms and sneered.

"Now you listen to me, insect," said the bully. "Hand it over, or I will squash you like a bug!"

The bully shook Toby roughly, the way he always did. And Toby, remembering the button on the vest concealed beneath his shirt, reached inside and pressed it.

The bully dropped Toby straight away, and his mouth attempted to scream. But the bully was so afraid, he had quite forgotten how.

From Toby's back sprouted great metal legs, which glistened even in the darkness of the alley. Each leg was ten feet long, and suddenly Toby towered over the bully, like a giant spider staring down at a fly.

Toby was just as surprised as the bully. The legs did whatever he wanted them to do. Toby had never felt so tall, or fast, or strong. It was the greatest feeling he had ever had, and as the boy stared down at the bully, he smiled.

"Now then, you villain!" cried Toby, courage in his voice. "Let's see who jingles!"

As the bully ran, he remembered how to scream. And as Toby chased him, he remembered how to laugh. He hadn't felt like laughing in a long, long time. His only regret was that aside from the bully, no one was there to hear it.

But Toby was wrong. As the boy chased the bully down the alley, someone did hear it—and see it, too.

Perched on a wall was a tiny metal fly. Its eyes focused mechanically as it watched the bully run. Its tiny ears perked up at the sound of Toby's laughter. And everything it saw, and everything it heard, it sent to Karl.

This was Karl's fly, which he had made just for the occasion. Safe and snug in his new shop, Karl saw everything the fly could see, and heard everything it could hear, through goggles and a helmet on his head.

Karl laughed and laughed and raised his arms in triumph. Toby had beaten the bully, with Karl's help, and he would never be bullied again.

Pim was happy too, and danced a little dance of victory.

THE PEAPOD

Karl had made a habit of having lunch at the park. He liked to go there to eat his sandwich and read his book and watch the children play, however briefly, in the tree.

He also liked to wave to the girl in the tower. Sometimes she would even wave back, though not very often. Karl thought the girl looked terribly sad. And he was right.

Karl had just finished his sandwich when the sun disappeared behind the tower. The children were all climbing down from the tree, but Karl thought he might stay for a bit and read. But just as he was opening his book, Miss Understood strode from her school and scooped up a little boy named Stuart.

"Aha! Got you, little piggy!" said Miss Understood. "And you will have a bath this very instant!"

Stuart was terribly dirty.

"No!" cried Stuart. "Anything but that!"

"Piggy has been rooting in the mud," said Miss Understood. "And we must clean him!"

"But the beast!" moaned Stuart. "The beast!"

"Poor little piggy doesn't like the water," said Miss Understood.

"Please!" wept Stuart in dismay. "Please don't make me!"

But try as he might, Stuart could not escape. Miss Understood was a stickler for cleanliness, even in such a dirty village. It was a hard job keeping the children clean, but Miss Understood had always been a hard worker. Still, Stuart was an especially difficult challenge, and she couldn't understand quite why.

As Miss Understood passed Karl, Stuart squirming in her arms, she sighed.

"I run his bath, I make the suds, and then I go

away," she said. "And every time, he screams and wails and runs and hides. I simply can't understand it. If only I could be a fly on the wall, just once!"

Wearing only a towel around his filthy waist, Stuart stood in a corner of the bathroom, his eyes wide with fright. The bath was steaming invitingly, and Stuart longed to step into the tub and wash away a layer or two of black soot. It was something he had even dreamt about, he wanted so much to be clean. Stuart loved baths.

But so did something else.

Stuart stared at the big, dark crack in the wall behind the tub. That's where the something else came from. And soon enough, it appeared.

It was a roach. It was the biggest roach Stuart had ever seen, and he had seen a great many. It was big, and it was mean, and it was white. And for some reason, every time Stuart was about to take his bath, the roach appeared and took it from him.

The roach climbed the side of the tub and slipped into the water. Stuart was very afraid, but he didn't want to disappoint Miss Understood. She wanted him to be clean. So with all the courage he could muster,

Stuart grasped a plunger. And holding it before him like a sword, he crept toward the tub and peered down into the suds. Perhaps he would catch the beast unawares, and plunge it away once and for all.

But just as Stuart peered down, the roach reared up and spit a great jet of water right in his face.

This was too much for poor Stuart. And dropping his plunger, he fled, right out the door and past Miss Understood, his towel dropping from his waist in the process.

As usual, Miss Understood didn't quite know what to make of that.

But even as Miss Understood went chasing after Stuart, a little fly rose from the bathroom wall and buzzed away out the window. Perhaps Miss Understood couldn't understand the mystery of the roach, but Karl could.

When Stuart awoke the next morning, he felt dirtier than ever. His nice clean sheets were gritty and black, and it was all the roach's fault. Stuart got up and sighed a heavy sigh. But then on his bedside table he found an unexpected thing.

It was a package, wrapped neatly in brown paper. And tied to the package with a little bit of string was a small card, which Stuart was quick to read.

With Kind Regards from K. Indergarten

That's what the little card said.

Stuart unwrapped the package and smiled. Someone had given him a tiny ship, and it was called the *Peapod*.

———————

Stuart ran a bath, steaming hot, and filled it with lots of suds. Once the tub was full, he placed the smart little ship on the water, where its metal sides and sails sparkled brightly. Then he stood back and waited for something to happen.

Soon enough, the awful roach appeared at its crack, crawled to the lip of the tub, and slipped into the water. It seemed bigger and meaner than ever, and Stuart shuddered with fear. Then he spied a movement aboard the ship.

From the ship's cabin emerged a crew of tiny metal men. Each man looked grim and courageous, and as they boarded small rowboats, then lowered them into the water, several gripped mighty harpoons. The tiny men quickly rowed to sea, and as they did, a final little man emerged from his quarters to watch.

This man wore a great beard and hat, and as he paced the decks of the *Peapod*, Stuart saw that one leg had gone missing, and been replaced by a stout metal peg. This man also clutched a harpoon, and Stuart knew he must surely be the captain.

The captain surveyed the sea, which was calm but distinctly foreboding.

The men in their rowboats were silent, awaiting the battle to come.

Then from the depths of the tub leapt the roach, soaring into the air and roaring a deafening roar.

"SHE BREACHES!" cried the captain.

Harpoons rained forth from the rowboats and stuck in the roach's hide. And as it dove back down, to scheme beneath the waves, water splashed from the tub.

The roach's plan was quite simple, and it didn't stay hidden for long. Swimming at great speed, it soon capsized one boat, and then another! As it turned in great circles, the sheer power of its passage made a whirlpool, in which the hapless sailors spun, praying to the sea gods for salvation.

The roach was having fun. And the captain didn't like that one bit.

As Stuart watched, his heart beating loudly in his chest, the roach swam straight for the *Peapod* at sickening speed. The ship would soon be rammed, and Stuart feared it would be sunk, along with his hopes for a bath.

But even as the great white roach bore down upon the ship, the mighty captain leapt from its deck, clutching his savage harpoon. And driving his spear down upon the roach, the prayers of his men were answered, as were Stuart's.

That was the end of the roach.

The capsized men returned to their rowboats. And as they hauled the roach to the side of the *Peapod*, triumphant in their victory, they sang a joyous song in celebration.

The sea she was a-boiling,
Yo ho, yo ho!
Our pants we were a-soiling,
Yo ho, yo ho!
But then the man with the mighty lance,
He slew the beast,

So let's change our pants,
And drink rum, rum, rum, rum,
Yo ho, yo ho, yo ho!

Stuart beamed at the captain. And when the tiny metal man saluted him, Stuart was quick to salute right back.

———————•———————

Karl was reading his book in the park when Stuart came walking by. Karl thought he had never seen such a clean little boy in all his life. In fact, he hardly recognized him. Stuart smiled and smiled. Today was a clean start for Stuart.

"I knew it!" said Miss Understood. "I just knew there was a little boy under all that grit and grime!"

Karl watched as Stuart ran off to play with the other children, while Miss Understood strode off to make lunch. Karl had things to do as well, back at his shop, and so he shut his book.

But when he did, he realized there was another little boy sitting beside him. The great big book had hidden him from view.

"Ah!" said Karl. "Hello."

"Hello," said the boy rather sadly. "My name is William."

"Hello, William," said Karl. "It seems you're sad."

"That's because I am," replied the boy.

"I see," said Karl. "Then we must render you un-sad, in order to restore your happiness."

"It is impossible," said William, "because everyone has a monster under their bed except for me."

"But monsters are abominable creatures, with fangs!" said Karl.

"And talons!" said William.

"And scales!"

"And horns!"

"And pointed tails and forked tongues!"

"And everyone has one but me!"

"I see," said Karl, pondering the matter. "So you actually *want* such a creature under your bed?"

"Absolutely," asserted William. "It would be my friend."

Before the conversation could continue, Miss Understood called out from the schoolhouse.

"Come, children," she yelled. "Lunch, and then geography! Don't put off till yesterday what you can do tomorrow!"

"It appears our cure shall have to be postponed," said Karl.

"That's okay," said William sadly. "Some problems just don't have a cure."

As the boy walked off, to lunch and then geography, Karl looked up at the tower. There was Agatha, standing in her window. It looked to Karl as if she might be crying.

And he was right.

CHAPTER 8

AGATHA'S ALLERGIES

Karl was busy working in his shop when in waddled Dr. Pimpledink, looking rather flummoxed. Like Miss Understood, Dr. Pimpledink had aged considerably over the years, but Karl still liked him quite a bit. Dr. Pimpledink was not an especially good doctor, but he was a good person. And to Karl, that was more important.

"Mr. Indergarten!" said Dr. Pimpledink. "I have a medical emergency of the most dire breed!"

"Whatever is the matter, Dr. Pimpledink?" asked Karl.

"My timepiece is in . . . time pieces," said the doctor. And with that, he withdrew from his pocket the pieces of his watch, on which he had mistakenly sat.

"My goodness!" said Karl. "I shall have to operate!"

"By all means, proceed!" replied the doctor.

As Karl undertook to repair the watch, Dr. Pimpledink looked on. Karl was very good at fixing watches, thought Dr. Pimpledink. To watch him with his tiny tools, it all looked so very easy. Sometimes, when someone is very good at something, it looks quite easy to other people—even if that something is quite difficult.

"You know, I envy you, Karl," said Dr. Pimpledink. "Deep within the bowels of your patients, gears and cogs all fit together as they should. Oh, you may adjust them slightly, perhaps oil them from time to time. And everything works very neatly. But people, Karl. People are very different. One simply never knows what makes them tick."

"Yes," said Karl, pausing briefly in his labors. "I've often wished I could . . . fix people."

"Imagine!" cried Dr. Pimpledink, throwing his arms in the air. "A little girl who's allergic to every-thing!"

Karl frowned. "No one is allergic to everything!"

"Ah, but she is," sighed the doctor. "The smell of marbles gives her migraines. New pajamas cause her pain. Crayons make her muscles cramp, and lentils make her lame. Knickers make her lymph nodes swell, fresh honey gives her hives. Kittens constipate her. It's true, I swear. No lie."

"Birthday cake and candles?"

"Meningitis, I'm afraid."

"And storybooks with pictures?"

"They make her heartbeat fade!"

"And you, Doctor?" asked Karl. "Surely she is not allergic to the sweet scent of care and concern!"

"Much to my dismay, I give her a fever of one hundred and three. In fact, the only thing she can possibly stomach is a cup of cucumber tea."

"But there must be something you can do!" gasped Karl in amazement.

"I've tried pills, potions, lotions, syrups, tonics, injections, and infusions," moaned Dr. Pimpledink. "I've consulted an acupuncturist, an aromatherapist, and an exorcist. I have written to esteemed physicians from every corner of the globe, and only one prescribed a solution: to remove her sense of smell."

"Then it must be done at once!" cried Karl.

"The technology is not yet available to us," said the doctor. "But he suggested she be frozen in a cryogenic chamber until such time as it is."

"How awful!"

"Her case has been the bane of my career," wept Dr. Pimpledink. "And the stress! I shouldn't wonder if I end up in hospital! Imagine explaining to the most powerful man in the village that his daughter's health is hopeless!"

Karl dropped the tool from his hand. The most powerful man in the village was Leopold Croak.

"What is your patient's name?" whispered Karl.

"Agatha," said Dr. Pimpledink. "Agatha Croak. And her condition is quite incurable, I'm afraid."

Agatha sat in her room, which was white. The walls were white. The floor was white. The bed was white. A dreary sight! Everything was white, and it was all scrubbed and disinfected three times daily, because Agatha was allergic to everything. Even toys.

This is a very unpleasant way for a little girl to live.

But there was one good thing about Agatha's life,

high in the tallest tower in town. And that was the view. Because Agatha's window looked straight down on the park, and the tree, and the man who sometimes waved to her.

For many, many years, in fact for as long as she could remember, Agatha had stood at the window and watched the children play, in the wonderful tree that seemed to slowly get smaller. Watching the children made Agatha very happy. And yet it made her sad at the very same time, which, as you know, is a curious way to feel.

Agatha had tried to talk to her father about the way she felt, especially the sad part. But he was usually too busy. He was a very important businessman.

Still, Leopold always did stop by, once a day, before his meetings began. If he had time, they might even chat a bit through the intercom at the door.

Today when Leopold buzzed at the door, Agatha peeped through the thick glass panel and saw that Grod was with him. Grod was the biggest person Agatha had ever seen, and she didn't like him one bit. Grod worked for her father. Grod never spoke, but he had a wicked laugh. Grod liked wicked things in general.

"Good morning, Agatha," came the voice at the intercom.

"Is it?" she sighed.

"Morning?" asked Leopold.

"Good."

"Indeed it is!" beamed Leopold. "Our stock value has soared with the news that Cuddlecom Incorporated will soon release a new and improved Emma. Preliminary estimates indicate that gross income will nearly triple in the first quarter alone."

Agatha said nothing. Agatha was not interested in corporate finance.

"I should think you'd be pleased," said her father.

Agatha shrugged and glanced at the window behind her.

"You've been watching those filthy children again!" said Leopold rather sternly.

"Only a little bit!" cried Agatha. "Only a little peek!"

"This is illogical, Agatha," said Leopold, "since watching them makes you sad."

"Oh, father!" wept Agatha. "You can't imagine how sad it makes me!"

"No," said Leopold. "I cannot."

And with that, he was off, to attend a series of

very important meetings. He would see to those filthy children who made his daughter sad. Yes, he would see to them first thing.

But as Leopold walked away, followed by the lumbering Grod, not he, or Grod, or even Agatha took note of the little fly, which rose from the window's small sill and buzzed away with the faintest whir of tiny gears and cogs.

CHAPTER 9

PROGRESS

The fly was Karl's of course, and with its help, he had seen and heard the whole exchange. Karl felt awfully bad for Agatha, but he just wasn't sure how to help. It was quite a pickle, and he would have to think on the matter at length. Meanwhile, it was time to steer his little spy back home.

The wind, however, had other plans entirely.

The wind blew hard and cold, and the tiny fly struggled against it. Karl, in his goggles and his helmet, worked the controls as best he could. But it was only a very little fly after all, and soon the wind took control entirely.

That's when something unexpected happened.

The wind blew the fly right through the big open window of a great big room—the boardroom of Cuddlecom Incorporated. There it landed on a great big table, surrounded by very important businessmen.

The fly looked around. Karl could see everything the fly could see. There was Leopold! And he was making a very important speech.

"Gentlemen!" said Leopold. "Public reaction to Cuddlecom's recent technological advances has proven overwhelming, particularly in America. And market research, as you well know, never lies."

The very important businessmen all nodded. Leopold was very smart, they thought.

"Progress, gentlemen, equals profit," he continued. "But in our quest for progress, sacrifices must be made. Our current manufacturing capabilities are, I regret to inform you, hopelessly inadequate. And in order to meet consumer demand, expansion is essential. Thus I am pleased to announce plans for a new facility, state of the art in every conceivable respect. This plant will dedicate itself entirely to production of our new prototype, with output of epic proportion."

The businessmen applauded. My goodness, Leopold was smart!

"Of course, real estate within the village is limited," said Leopold, "but progress waits for no man! And so we shall break ground on virgin soil, wasted to date on idle recreation. Gentlemen, I am pleased to inform you that we shall build our factory in the park!"

There was a pause. No one applauded at that. The park was the last place left for the children, and some of the children belonged to some of the businessmen.

"But Mr. Croak," said one of the businessmen. "It seems to me the park isn't really ours to take, given the needs of the children. My own daughter plays there, you know."

But Leopold had thought of that already.

"My plans do not ignore the children," said Leopold. "Indeed, the children are our future! For it is they who shall work at our factory!"

"But Mr. Croak!" cried the businessmen.

"They're cheaper!" cried Leopold.

"But!"

"They're meeker!"

"But!"

"And best of all," said Leopold with a sinister grin, "they do as they're told."

Then Grod saw the fly. And with one big hand, he squashed it.

Karl removed his goggles and his helmet, and turned to Pim.

"Oh, Pim!" he cried. "This is all my fault!"

Pim shook his head back and forth. It didn't seem like Karl's fault to Pim.

"Oh, but it is!" said Karl. "For it was I who made him walk the plank!"

Pim didn't know what Karl was talking about. But when Karl stood up and grabbed his tiny tools, Pim could tell he had a plan. So Pim followed excitedly as Karl strode to the back of the shop and lifted a trap door in the floor. There, rough stairs led down, deep into the cavernous village sewers. No one ever went down there. But that's just where Karl was going.

"Come on then, Pim," said Karl with a smile. "Perhaps you'll have a romance with a sewer rat!"

Pim didn't like the sound of that at all, and made a nasty face. Yuck!

"Some rats are evil, Pim," sighed Karl. "I won't argue that. But they're almost never born that way."

And this is true—of rats, of cats, of dogs, and everything else. It's especially true of people.

So Karl and Pim climbed down, deep into the sewers, and the trap door shut softly behind them.

CHAPTER 10

EMMA OBEYS

The next day, Leopold strode through the village, the massive Grod following close behind. But people didn't bow and smile politely, the way they usually did when Leopold was around. Word had spread, you see, of Leopold's wicked plan. And now people grumbled and frowned.

Leopold didn't care one bit. He had more important things to think about, and he checked his fancy watch to make sure he was on schedule.

He was most annoyed when Miss Understood appeared to delay him.

"Leopold Croak!" she cried, with a voice that boomed like thunder.

There she was, at the end of the street. The crowd parted right down the middle, so everyone could see what was happening. Leopold stared at Miss Understood, and Miss Understood stared right back, with eyes like burning embers.

In her hand was a yardstick, which she held before her as she approached her former pupil.

"And so!" she said. "You would put the children to work!"

Leopold glanced around him. Everyone did seem rather upset. They were all being quite illogical in his opinion.

"I would give them opportunity," said Leopold. "A chance at a fair wage, a better life."

"And what of their playtime, and their schooling?" demanded Miss Understood.

"Playime is time wasted," said Leopold. "And education is a worthless commodity. There is no profit in it."

"And your tree, Leopold?" said Miss Understood. "Do you care nothing for your tree?"

"It stands in the way of progress," replied Leopold.

Now Miss Understood got angry, angrier than

she had ever been in her life. Leopold was being very naughty, and she simply wouldn't stand for it. The situation called for drastic measures.

"Never, in all my years," said Miss Understood, "have I ever punished a child with my stick. But today, Leopold Croak, you shall be the first."

With that, she gave his hand a smart little slap with her ruler. Slap!

Leopold's hand wasn't hurt in the slightest, but his pride was. Leopold Croak was a very important person, after all, and not accustomed to being punished in any way, shape, or form, let alone in front of a crowd.

So Leopold didn't care for the slap one bit, and neither did Grod. Grod stepped forward, looking very cruel, and stared down at Miss Understood with a terrifying glare.

But Miss Understood wasn't frightened at all.

"This is how I taught you?" she asked of Leopold. "To hide behind your ape?"

Leopold considered and checked his watch. He was running quite behind schedule, to be sure, but with all these people about, it simply wouldn't do to have Grod push an old woman into the mud. That could be bad for public relations. No, thought Leopold, he would have to deal with this himself.

So Leopold stepped forward from behind the giant Grod, and spoke in no uncertain terms.

"Now you listen to me," he said to Miss Understood.

But before he could continue, she gave his hand two smart little slaps with her ruler. Slap, slap!

"I put this town on the map!" cried Leopold.

His cry was met with three more slaps, slightly harder than the last ones. Slap, slap, slap!

"And I will not be cowed," yelled Leopold, whose pride was now deeply injured, "by a haggard old crone bearing a stick!"

The crowd gasped. No one had ever said anything like that to Miss Understood. The embers in her eyes turned to flame as she raised her yardstick in the air. And then came such a flurry of little slaps that Leopold had to raise his arms to protect himself.

Slap, slap, slap, slap, slap! And then, a crunch.

The crowd gasped again. Miss Understood paused, breathing heavily, and teetered on her feet. Suddenly, Miss Understood did not look well at all.

Leopold looked down at his watch, which was broken. He looked at the watch, and then at Miss

Understood, and frowned a hideous frown. It had been a very fancy watch, and Leopold was most displeased. But Miss Understood stared back at him, now with only love in her eyes.

"The apple," she gasped, "doesn't fall far . . . from me."

And with that, she collapsed in the street.

Dr. Pimpledink rushed forward, waddling just as fast as he could waddle. Kneeling heavily on both knees, he listened close at Miss Understood's chest.

"It's her heart," said Dr. Pimpledink. "Quite incurable, I'm afraid."

As the crowd surged forward to help, Leopold turned to Grod and said a terrible thing.

"Progress favors the strong."

Karl was standing behind the counter of his shop when in walked Leopold Croak. Long, long ago, the two had been best friends. But now Karl wasn't sure the man even recognized him. Karl thought that Leopold looked very different, now that he was so important. He certainly didn't look like a friend anymore. In fact, he looked like an enemy. Leopold was the first and only enemy Karl had ever had.

Leopold didn't think of Karl as a friend, or as an enemy. He had just read the bright gold letters on the window of the shop, and now he simply thought of Karl as someone who might fix his watch. So he placed it on the counter and shrugged.

"Irreparable, I suspect," said Leopold.

Karl thought about all the things he wanted to say to Leopold. Some of them were rather nasty, to be sure. But Karl didn't like saying nasty things. So rather than saying anything at all, he decided to work on the watch. He was much better at fixing watches than he was at talking anyway.

But Leopold was very good at talking, and as he strode about the shop, he said a great many interesting things.

"An exact science, time," he said, "from a numerical perspective. I am a devout student of precision. I find that while few appreciate its subtleties, most will pay handsomely for its rewards. Truth be told, our professions are not so very different, yours and mine. We are both . . . vendors of precision, shall we say."

Karl briefly considered saying that in fact he didn't agree, but Leopold was already talking again.

"Soon enough," said he, "the world will meet the successor to Emma Cuddles, courtesy of Cuddlecom Incorporated. And my engineers assure me, she shall surpass every consumer expectation."

Leopold's voice rose as he spoke. He seemed very excited about surpassing consumer expectations.

"Every toy store on the planet will be mobbed!" he cried. "Every wallet will be emptied! And every last ear on earth will echo with the name . . . *Emma Obeys.*"

The name indeed echoed in Karl's little shop. Leopold was feeling very dramatic and important. He stared hard at Karl, hoping for a reaction—and possibly even applause. But Karl was busy working on the watch. It almost seemed to Leopold that Karl wasn't listening. Sometimes this happened, Leopold knew, among unimportant people. They weren't as smart as he was, and didn't always know when something important was being said.

It was then that Leopold noticed the book on Karl's counter. It was very large and impressive. And on its cover was the title:

Anatomy of the Human Brain

How strange, thought Leopold, that a clockmaker should be interested in brains. Leopold considered himself a great expert on brains. And his favorite brain, other than his own, was the brain of Emma Obeys.

"Her intelligence, while admittedly artificial," said Leopold, "remains a testament to the heroic march of technology. As our advertising suggests, she is an absolute marvel, obedient to her master in every conceivable respect—just as the consumer is obedient to me."

Karl still wasn't listening. What a bland and unimportant little man, thought Leopold, who couldn't even get excited about technology. What a waste of such a very fine speech. He would have to leave straight away and find a better audience.

"So tell me," sighed Leopold, referring to his watch, "can it be fixed?"

Karl held forward the watch.

Tick. Tock. Tick. Tock.

It was working just like new, and Leopold was very surprised.

"Well," he said. "Imagine that."

With that, he placed a large gold coin on the counter and strode from the shop in search of better company.

Pim leapt from Karl's pocket and ran for the secret trap door. Pim had heard everything, of course, and knew that Leopold was up to no good.

Karl knew it, too. And together, they descended into the darkness, the name of Emma Obeys still sounding faintly in their ears.

CHAPTER 11

BACKHOES AND BLOOMERS

Agatha had risen very early, awakened by a menacing rumble. Rushing to her window, she was stricken by what she saw.

Huge trucks were converging at the edge of the park, and on each truck was a great machine of destruction. There were cranes and backhoes and bulldozers, and all sorts of other things designed for digging and mashing and gnashing. Workmen were unloading the machines and pouring fuel into their engines.

Agatha knew at once what they were going to
do. They were going to destroy the park. Before she
ever had a chance to play there. Before she ever had a
chance to climb the tree. The tree seemed to know it,
too. And as Agatha stared down, a single leaf fell from
the tree and floated slowly to the ground.

Now there was only one left.

If only she could run and stop them. But she
couldn't. Because Agatha was allergic to everything,
except for cucumber tea.

She could only stand at her lonely little window and
watch. And as she did, she saw her father.

***

Leopold strolled toward the park. Behind him walked
Grod, who was excited about the machines. Grod liked
destruction, though he preferred to do it himself.

At Leopold's side tottered Emma Obeys, the very
first Emma Obeys to totter off the assembly line.
Emma Obeys was very lifelike, almost like a real
little girl. But while she did have a sort of brain,
she did not have a heart. And so you must understand, Emma Obeys was just a doll. She would never
be a real little girl, no matter what. Yet as she

tottered along, walking at Leopold's side, the man was very pleased to note that Emma Obeys was not allergic to anything.

To Leopold, Emma Obeys seemed perfect. And as he strode forward, he smiled to himself at the amazement of the workmen. Soon, he knew, all the world would be amazed, and he would be richer than ever.

"My goodness me," said Leopold, so everyone could hear. "Progress does make one rather thirsty! Emma, would you be so kind as to fetch me a refreshment?"

Straight away, the doll trotted off to find a thermos, and the men all oohed and aahed as she poured a black cup of coffee.

"No, no, Emma," scolded Leopold. "You know how I take my coffee—like our future together."

At this, Emma poured a great deal of sugar in the coffee and stirred it with her finger.

"That's right, Emma," smiled Leopold. "Sweet."

The foreman then stepped forward to offer Leopold an update.

"Should be ready by tomorrow, guv'nor," he said. "I've got the lads workin' triple shifts."

"That is satisfactory," replied Leopold. "And what time might we commence?"

"Well before dawn, Mr. Croak, if you like."

"Excellent," said Leopold. "Time is money, you know."

"Yes sir, Mr. Croak."

"Tomorrow dawns a new day in the global economy," said Leopold. "In fact, make a note of that, Emma. We shouldn't want to miss our appointment with . . . destiny."

As Emma Obeys produced a pad and pencil, and quickly scribbled a note, Leopold watched her with pride. She was perfect. She was the future. She was almost, in some ways, like a daughter.

"Plastics, gentlemen!" he cried. "We shall forge our future in plastics!"

⸺•⸺

Karl watched the trucks, and Emma Obeys, from the shadow of an alley, and wondered if he could possibly feel any worse. Then he looked up at the little window in the tower and saw Agatha.

Yes, it was definitely possible to feel worse.

Try as he might, Karl was stumped. How could he help a little girl who was allergic to everything? It was impossible. It was tragic. And thinking it over, right then and there, Karl decided that when it came to Agatha Croak, he was a failure.

So Karlheinz Indergarten, the great big failure, waved a final time to Agatha, the girl he had failed, and walked away. Agatha watched as he melted into the alley and disappeared. It felt like he was saying goodbye.

As Karl walked, he kicked an empty tin can. And as the wind blew chill against him, he pulled his collar high against the cold.

That's when something unexpected happened.

A great big pair of ladies' underwear flew right in Karl's face, courtesy of the powerful wind. It was so big, it covered his head.

Karl removed the underwear, which was slightly damp, and stared at it. It had little blue flowers printed all over, front and back. Karl thought the flowers rather pretty.

"Degenerate!" hissed a voice.

Karl turned to find a fat little washerwoman trotting right for him. And judging by the washerwoman's expansive circumference, Karl rightly guessed that the underwear was hers.

Snatching the bloomers back with a sinister snarl,

the washerwoman quickly returned to her clothesline, strung at the back of her shack. There she grabbed a thick wooden clothespin in her thick little fingers and hung her undies to dry.

The clothespin pinched down, snug and tight, right where it was supposed to pinch. Karl pinched himself to be sure he wasn't dreaming. Then he blew a kiss, straight to the fat little washerwoman, and ran off. He and Pim had a great deal of work to do.

The washerwoman was flattered, though Karl was not her type. She liked her men short and fat.

CHAPTER 12

JUST LIKE CLOCKWORK

Now. It was always dark in the village because of the soot and the smog. But on this particular morning, it was raining, which meant it was even darker than usual. Leopold had risen very early to watch the destruction of the park, and so had Grod. Grod was very excited and hoped there might be explosions.

Emma Obeys had not exactly risen, because she never slept. She had just stared blankly, all night long, waiting to obey someone.

Leopold, Grod, and Emma Obeys walked from the doors of Cuddlecom Incorporated, Grod holding an umbrella above them. The rain pitter-pattered down from above, and when they reached the park, the workmen all came forward. The foreman was holding a shovel, which he offered to Leopold with tremendous pomp and formality.

"It's custom, guv'nor," said he. "The chief always breaks ground first, with no exceptions. Can't imagine what the men might think if we did otherwise."

"Neither can I," said Leopold, and took the shovel.

Leopold stared hard at the men, and then at the tree, and its single, sad little leaf. Soon, the tree would be gone, and he could build his factory. Then the children couldn't play, and they wouldn't make Agatha sad. And they would all be very rich, richer than ever before, which Leopold hoped might make his daughter happy. It was all very logical to Leopold.

Leopold raised the shovel high in the air, then thrust it down, deep into the mud at his feet. And with a terrible cry, he yelled.

"Let the future begin!"

The backhoes and bulldozers rumbled and grumbled to life. And the earth shook beneath them in fear.

William was asleep in his bed when he felt the first slight tremor. His eyes came slightly open, and he wondered what on earth it might have been.

But there was only silence, and William's groggy eyes soon shut again in slumber.

Then came another tremor, greater than the first, from just beneath his bed. William sat bolt upright and guessed straight away just what it was.

"There's a monster under my bed."

The other children were still asleep. Toby was snoring a bit, and Stuart was dreaming of ships.

Then the floorboards cracked, right under William's bed, and the children came awake with a start. William stared at them all, and his eyes were wide with joy.

"There's a monster under my bed!"

The children stared at one another, and then at William. This was a very unusual way to start the day.

Then William's bed began to hop about like a bucking bronco, as something pushed and pushed again from underneath. William held on, like a brave and strapping cowboy, and smiled from ear to ear. And as the other children ran to huddle in a corner of the room, the cowboy cried out in triumph.

"THERE'S A MONSTER UNDER MY BED!"

The bed then flew across the room, and William tumbled into the corner, to stand with his friends as the monster burst from the floor.

It was a dragon. A clockwork dragon. It was the biggest dragon in the history of dragons, which is a very long history indeed. And as it stared down at the children, its metal fangs, and talons and scales and horns and tail and tongue, shone golden, even in the darkness.

The children didn't quite know what to make of that.

The dragon stretched its neck, bursting through the roof. Bits of wood and plaster rained down upon the children, and William held his breath in silent rapture.

Then the dragon bent down to look at William. And with one mechanical eye, it winked.

William winked right back.

As the dragon leapt into the sky, spreading its great metal wings, a little paper card floated down from high above, right into William's outstretched hand.

With Kind Regards from K. Indergarten

That's what the little card said.

When Miss Understood appeared in her nightgown, she was most perplexed.

———————•———————

The dragon soared into the sky, glistening in the thick soot and smog. It glanced to the ocean, close in the west, then turned its gaze to the park. Far below, the backhoes and bulldozers had just begun their assault.

As the dragon dove, fast and straight as an arrow, the foreman looked up and screamed. The other workmen followed his gaze and trembled at what they saw. A great, dark shadow was hurtling down from the heavens, and with it came dread and doom. When a bolt of lightning flashed, illuminating the great, golden dragon for just an instant, the workmen all fled in fear.

The dragon landed, heavy and glorious, with a thud that rocked the village. There it stood, ten tons of perfect clockwork, to defend the sad little tree.

The dragon paused to eye the great machines, which didn't seem so very great to him at all. And with one savage lash of its massive clockwork tail, the dragon sent a bulldozer flying, to crash into a factory.

And Leopold looked on, with narrowed eyes, as his dream became a nightmare.

Meanwhile, Pim was running just as fast as his feet would carry him, a little package tied to his tail. When the crashes came from the park in the distance, his whiskers twitched with pleasure. Karl's great plan had begun.

But Pim failed to notice that as he passed an alley, a pair of glowing eyes came alight—and quickly followed.

The dragon crushed a crane in its jaws, then stomped on a great big truck. Backhoes sailed from the park, to land far away in the muck.

The air was thick with machinery. Grod was glad he'd brought an umbrella.

Pim was startled when the alley cat appeared before him, grinning a mischievous grin. He skidded to an immediate halt and wondered just what to do.

Run. Yes, that was the thing to do. And so he ran, even faster than before, the package tied to his tail bouncing along just after.

As the alley cat gave chase, it was joined by its feline friends.

———————

The dragon looked about. He'd done an awfully good job. The machines had all been destroyed, and with them a number of factories. In fact, just about everything had been destroyed altogether, except the park. And the tree, which for the time being was safe.

Leopold frowned. This was not the sort of destruction he'd had in mind.

Then the dragon turned to stare at Leopold.

———————

Pim ran and ran, trying hard to get to the tower. But the cats were close behind and quickly gaining.

Pim vaulted a trash can and turned on a dime. He redoubled his efforts. There wasn't much time.

Then he took a very wrong turn and found himself trapped at the end of a very long alley, where a tall brick wall stood in wait.

The alley cats approached and drew their claws.

———————

With grave and ominous intent, the dragon plodded toward Leopold, who stood with Grod and Emma Obeys.

Leopold hated the dragon. The dragon didn't much like Leopold, either.

———◆———

Pim began to tremble. The alley cats approached, their green eyes glowing in the murk. Pim clawed at the brick walls, slippery with rain, and knew that he could never climb them.

So he turned to face the band of brigands, now hissing with vicious intent. He would fight as best he could and fall quite nobly in battle.

It came as quite a surprise to all assembled when the dog leapt over the cats, from out of nowhere, to stand in Pim's defense.

This was the dog that Karl had fed when he first returned to the village. At the time, as you'll recall, Pim had scolded the dog for its manners.

But now the dog was different. He was a very good dog after all.

Yet still, with strength in numbers, the cats were not afraid. The dog's thick hackles rose from its neck as it bared its sharp, white teeth. Soon, the dog thought, he just might howl with rage. So he took a very deep breath in preparation.

Swift as a viper, the dragon lowered its head, just inches away, to look Leopold right in the eye.

Then it roared the loudest roar ever roared.

The roar burst forth like a wave, washing over Leopold, Grod, and Emma Obeys with the force of a thousand storms.

The remaining factory windows shuddered, then shattered, and finally fell tinkling to the ground.

When the cats heard the roar, they leapt ten feet in fright.

They thought the roar had come from the dog, who was, in his own way, now roaring.

The cats decided promptly to retreat. And as they sped away, to hide from the terrible dog that roared like a dragon, the actual roar came to a sudden stop.

The dog turned to Pim and offered him a paw. Pim was glad to shake it, for he had made a friend.

The dog watched happily as Pim ran off, his little package in tow. The dog felt very good about himself. He hadn't made a friend in some time.

The dragon raised its head to tower again over Leopold. He hadn't quite considered what might follow his mighty roar.

The dragon was thusly very surprised when Leopold turned to the doll at his side and said quite calmly, "Emma? Please attack."

Emma Obeys tottered toward the dragon. The dragon thought this must be some sort of joke. But on came the awful little doll, looking altogether horrid and heartless.

So the dragon lifted one great foot and crushed it, flat as a pancake.

The dragon grinned at Leopold. He would have to do better than that.

Leopold breathed very deep, and then yelled very loud.

"I BELIEVE I SAID, 'ATTACK!'"

And then came the hordes, hordes of Emma Obeys, streaming from the broken factory windows like ten thousand angry ants.

As the dragon watched, in both disgust and disbelief, the swarm came quickly toward him, climbing his great legs and tail.

He shook them off and roared again, but on the army came.

The dragon stomped with its feet and lashed out with its mighty tail. Hundreds of dolls were squished and squashed, and sent sailing into the sky. But always there were more, climbing and biting and pinching and punching, and pulling at the dragon's clockwork hide.

Once again, Grod was very glad to have brought an umbrella, as the dolls rained down from above.

———•———

Agatha had seen it all. She had seen the dragon burst from the school and descend to defend the tree. She had seen the dragon's triumph, and heard its mighty roar.

It was, considered Agatha, the greatest thing she'd ever seen. It was the finest day she'd ever had. But her day was about to get better.

That's when Agatha heard the sound of a tiny clockwork mouse, squeezing under the door. It was Pim.

"Hello!" said Agatha.

Pim held forth the package. It was neatly wrapped in brown paper and tied up with a bit of string.

"Oh, but I mustn't!" said Agatha. "I'm allergic to brown paper packages tied up with string!"

But Pim was very insistent. It seemed very important to the little mouse that Agatha open the package. Then Agatha noticed the tiny paper card, which she quickly lifted to read. The rain had made the card rather soggy, and the ink had run in rather wayward directions. But using just a little imagination, Agatha found that she could just make out the blurry words.

"With kind regards," whispered Agatha, "from . . . Kindergarten."

Kindergarten! That must be the man who waved sometimes, thought Agatha, and read his book in the park! The little clockwork mouse was his, and that meant the dragon was, too!

Agatha was right of course, being quite a clever little girl. Karl had built the dragon deep down in the sewers, where no one ever went, and his clockwork mouse had helped him.

Agatha opened the package, and when she did, she smiled. Her face shone fierce and golden, not unlike the dragon's, and for the very first time in her life, Agatha Croak felt like roaring.

The dragon tried and tried, but the dolls were far too many. Every time he squished or squashed an Emma, ten more would rush to take its place. The dragon was covered in them now, little plastic, heartless dolls that squirmed and pulled at his scales.

This was a battle the dragon could not win.

So the dragon stretched its wings again and leapt into the sky. High above the village, it twisted and turned in the air, and shook its mighty bulk from stem to stern. But the little heartless dolls held on, loyal to their master.

When lightning struck the dragon, the dolls were set aflame.

Yet even as they burned, they still attacked.

There on the dragon they melted and seeped between its scales, jamming the gears and cogs protected deep within.

The dragon looked down and spied William, who stared up at him through the rain. The dragon soon would fall, but he refused to fall on his boy.

So with one final wink, which William would always remember, the dragon soared toward the ocean. The dragon had fought bravely and had tried to make his boy proud. The dragon's heart was filled with joy to think of William, and ticked and tocked with love.

But when the molten plastic reached his heart, the ticking slowed, then came to a stop. And thus the dragon fell.

William cried out for his monster, and Miss Understood rushed to his side. There she knelt by the boy and hugged him as tight as she could. But even as William cried in her arms, a cruel sound crept into his ears.

It was Grod. He was laughing.

Leopold wasn't angry. Instead, he was simply confused. The entire day had proven most illogical.

Where had the dragon come from? Why would someone build it at all? Leopold, after all, was striving very hard for progress. Progress was a good thing, maybe even the best thing, considered Leopold. Why would someone build a dragon to stand in its way?

Everywhere he looked, he saw delays to his schedule. His machines had all been ruined, as had his first batch of Emma Obeys, though a few still tottered here and there. Several factories had crumbled and fallen, and Leopold knew he'd have to pay his workmen overtime to clean everything up. Overtime would put a big dent in his profits.

And there, amidst the wreckage, and the bodies of Emma Obeys, stood the tree.

The tree, which reminded him of his boyhood, when he was so very poor. The tree, which still had one green leaf and defied his one great dream.

Leopold hated the tree.

But as he stared at the tree, and hated all for which it still stood, a small warm hand reached up to take his own. Leopold looked down.

"Agatha!"

Yes, it was Agatha. And on the very end of her nose was a beautiful golden clothespin. A nosepin!

"But Agatha!" gasped Leopold. "Your allergies!"

"But I'm absolutely fine, Father!" cried the delighted Agatha. "For I cannot smell a thing!"

For just a moment, Leopold paused. For just a second, he almost smiled. But still, there stood the tree. And until the tree was gone, he could not give Agatha her future, and all the riches that would come with it.

Thus the smile faded and turned to a sinister frown.

"You are about to learn a valuable lesson," said Leopold to his daughter. "Progress in the face of adversity. Your timing, I must say, is impeccable."

"Just like clockwork!" said Agatha in delight.

"Clockwork!" gasped Leopold.

And then he knew, just like that, who had made the dragon.

Leopold strode quickly to Grod and whispered something awful in his ear. Grod laughed and lumbered off, as Agatha's heart skipped two beats.

"Where is he going?" asked Agatha, though she had already guessed.

"To remove an obstacle," hissed Leopold, turning to the tree. "Just as we are going to do."

CHAPTER 13

INCURABLE YET AGAIN

Karl was sitting in his shop, working with his tiny tools. He stared through a magnifying glass as he used them, because his newest creations were so very small that even he could barely see them.

They looked like itsy-bitsy bugs, and they were nearly finished.

Karl squinted his eyes and, ever so carefully, lifted the final little bug with his tiny pair of tweezers. It was beautiful, possibly even perfect. He placed it in a golden orb, on a bed of rich black velvet, next to its many brothers and sisters. And then he sighed and smiled, remembering the words of his wonderful friend the clockmaker.

"It's the little things that have the most potential."

Karl closed the orb. The latch locked tightly in place with a very satisfactory sound, and Karl stared at the inscription he had carved in its golden shell.

That's when Pim rushed in and scampered right up Karl's leg to the workbench. At first, Karl thought that Pim was simply dancing. But no, he quickly realized, Pim was doing a pantomime. And clearly, Pim was scared.

Pim swelled his tiny chest and rose to his full height, then lumbered about like a giant.

"Gargantuan!" guessed Karl straight away.

Pim nodded and nodded again, then grasped a heavy pair of cutting shears and placed his tail between the blades.

Karl frowned and grimaced.

"Gruesome!" he rightly guessed.

Pim nodded again, then donned a thimble for a hat. And pulling it low over his eyes, he walked toward Karl with a very cruel look indeed. For just a moment, Karl thought Pim meant to hurt him. But Pim would never do that.

"Goon!" cried Karl. And Pim did a quick little

somersault, to show his best friend that he was right.

Karlheinz Indergarten didn't quite know what to make of that.

Then a shadow loomed at the window, and the front door burst from the shop, cleanly ripped from its moorings.

There stood Grod. And at the awful sight of him, Pim turned tail and dove right in Karl's pocket.

Karl grasped the orb. At all costs, Grod must never have it.

Grod eyed the doorframe. It was so small, and he was so big, there was no way he could get in. So with one big fist, hard and strong as a sledgehammer, he struck the doorframe's timbers, which splintered and fell to the floor.

In strode Grod. As he walked, he hammered the walls. The beautiful clocks were all crushed, never to tick-tock again. But Karl didn't care, so long as he still held the orb. The orb was the only thing that mattered now. It mattered even more than Karl himself, or so he thought at the time.

The trap door! The secret door! Maybe Karl could reach it! He would have to be fast, very fast, fast as a bolt of lightning. So Karl turned and ran.

And yet, Grod was faster.

Just as Karl knelt to pull the ring on the little trap door, Grod was upon him. As Karl looked up, a mighty fist came hurtling down. And the clockmaker knew no more.

When Karl hit the ground, the orb rolled slowly to a corner of the shop. And as Grod laughed and laughed and laughed, Pim scurried from Karl's pocket and hid behind a broom.

Grod tied Karl in rope, from his neck right down to his toes, and heaved him over one huge shoulder. Leopold had told Grod to rid the village of clock-makers, and Grod was happy to do so. Grod liked hitting people, and laughing at them even better.

But before Grod could quite leave the shop, a small figure appeared at the door to block his passage.

"You will put him down this instant!" roared brave little Agatha Croak. Her voice rang clear and true, even with the clothespin on her nose.

Yet on came Grod, as if no one were there at all.

"My name is Agatha Croak, and you are in the service of my father!"

On walked the gargantuan goon, a gruesome look in his eyes.

"I will not let you take Kindergarten!" cried Agatha. And boy, did she ever mean it.

Grod stood before her, full twenty times her size, and raised a hand.

Agatha shut her eyes.

Then, just as gently as can be, Grod plucked the pin from Agatha's nose and walked out, to toss it high on a rooftop.

Agatha opened her eyes and remembered: She was allergic to everything.

⎯⎯⎯⎯⎯⎯⎯

The clothespin sat on the rooftop, far from Agatha's nose. Then a little boy knelt down, bending each of his ten-foot legs to do so, and picked it up.

It was Toby. He was wearing his special vest, that had been given him with kind regards. Toby only used his vest in great emergencies, like a superhero. But when Toby saw the dragon fall, he knew this was one of those times. He had been scuttling and leaping among the village rooftops ever since, and he had seen the evil Grod as he went about his business. It was clearly time to do heroic things.

Toby leapt from the rooftop, clothespin in hand,

and when he landed, he commanded his big metal legs to retract. Snickety-snick! They disappeared at once. Toby ran toward Karl's shop, and there he met Stuart, who was standing over Agatha. Stuart had a satchel slung over one shoulder, and he was looking very serious.

"It's the little girl from the tower," said Stuart. "She's sick."

It was true. Agatha's eyes were closed, and she was trembling. All her terrible allergies were attacking her at once. But Toby knew what to do, and he clamped her nose tight shut with the golden clothespin Karl had made.

Agatha sat up with a start and cried out. "Kindergarten!"

Toby and Stuart glanced at each other and didn't know quite what to say. Sometimes they felt shy around pretty little girls.

"They've taken him!" said Agatha. "And now it's all up to us!"

You see, Agatha knew full well that lacking an experienced protagonist like Karl, it now fell to her to lead the charge. Normal people are sometimes forced to do such things in a pinch, a circumstance commonly referred to as "rising to the occasion."

Then there was a very curious sound, like a bowling ball rolling fast down its alley. As the children turned to look, Karl's golden orb came rolling toward them.

Pim had done the rolling. And when the little clockwork mouse stepped out from behind the orb, Agatha knew him at once.

"Hello again!" said Agatha. With that she picked up the orb and read the inscription on its side. As she did, her eyes grew wide in wonder. Agatha knew what to do.

"I must get to the tree at once," she said, "if only there's still time!"

Snickety-snick! Toby's powerful metal legs sprouted from his back, lickety-split.

"Leave that to me!" said Toby, quite heroically. And reaching for Agatha with one great leg, he placed her astride his back. Stuart thought it a wonderful sight. A pretty little girl riding a spider!

But Agatha looked down at Stuart and spoke very solemn words.

"It's up to you to save Kindergarten," said she.

"All by myself?" asked Stuart.

"Of course not!" snapped Agatha, rolling her eyes.

And with that, Pim bounded right up Stuart's leg and stood ready on his shoulder.

"But which way do we go?" demanded the boy.

"TO THE SEA!"

Everyone looked down. Peeping from Stuart's satchel was a tiny metal man, holding a spyglass to his eye.

It was the captain.

⸺•⸺

Grod had long since reached the harbor. There he found a huge freighter, just preparing to head to sea. It was bound for America, far across the ocean, and that seemed just fine to Grod. So with one powerful arm, he tossed Karl high up the freighter's side, where he landed in a lifeboat, still unconscious. Grod had hit him very hard, you see, and knocked the consciousness right out of him.

The freighter blew its big shrill whistle. Toot toot! Thus it pulled from the dock and steamed very slowly to sea.

Grod put his hands on his hips and laughed. That was the last of the clockmaker. Leopold would be very pleased. Grod might even get a bonus in his paycheck.

If he did, he thought, he would buy himself a fancy club. Hitting people with a good club sounded very fine to Grod.

Whoosh! Something very small came whistling through the air and stuck right in Grod's big leg. Grod looked down.

It was a tiny harpoon.

Grod turned. There stood a little boy, and on his shoulder was a mouse. This was very curious. But even more curious was the tiny metal man standing on the little boy's satchel. The man wore a great beard and hat, and one of his legs had gone missing, and been replaced by a stout metal peg.

The captain had thrown the harpoon. He looked very pleased with himself.

Grod rolled up his sleeves and cracked his great big knuckles. No one was going to harpoon Grod and get away with it, that was certain.

That's when something unexpected happened.

High atop a stack of wooden crates appeared William, staring coldly down at Grod.

"Get him," said William, with fire in his eyes.

There was a long, dramatic pause.

"I SAID," roared William, "GET HIM!"

From behind the wooden crates ran fifty plastic dolls, straight for Grod. These were the last of Emma Obeys, the only awful dolls to survive the dragon's wrath. William had secretly rounded them up, like a sort of miniature plastic posse. And because Leopold had ceased to issue any orders whatsoever, except to Grod, the dolls were now quite contentedly under William's command.

The dolls climbed right up Grod's huge legs and punched and punched away. When he tried to cover his face, they punched his belly. When he tried to cover his belly, they punched his face. They punched very hard, thought Grod, for such very little dolls. His only hope was to run far, far away.

But even as he ran, the dolls kept punching.

"That's for my monster!" cried William, and he meant it with all his heart.

Grod ran and continued to run until he had left the village, and then the province, and then the country. The dolls continued to punch him, though, until Grod found a kindly doctor in a place called Yugoslavia who was able to remove them surgically. There Grod became religious and decided that punching was a wicked thing to do.

Stuart and William stared out to sea, at the freighter bound for America.

"We're too late," said William sadly.

But Stuart opened his satchel and removed his tiny toy ship, the *Peapod*. Preparations for the journey were already underway, as the crew climbed the rigging to unfurl the ship's small sails.

The captain stood on the deck and looked up at the boy with a grin.

"You must save Kindergarten," said Stuart.

"Aye," came the staunch reply. "That we will."

Stuart placed the ship on the water, where it bobbed very smartly, as it should. Pim leapt aboard with great courage, and his whiskers twitched with excitement as he eyed the horizon ahead. There, somewhere far away, awaited Karl.

"Goodbye, Captain," sighed Stuart, tears welling in his eyes. "I will miss you."

"Captain?" exclaimed the tiny metal man. "But I'm only the first mate, my boy! *You're* the captain!"

With that, the whole crew, and Pim as well, saluted Stuart. And more proud than he had ever been before, Stuart saluted right back.

As the ship set sail that day, leaving Stuart and

William behind, the fearless crew ventured ever farther
to sea. The wind came strong behind them, filling their
sails and their hearts with hope. And as they sailed, in
search of Karlheinz Indergarten, they sang as only true
sailors can sing.

Adventure lies before us,
Yo ho, yo ho!
The salt air washes o'er us,
Yo ho, yo ho!
We leave behind our hearth and house,
To brave the waves with a clockwork mouse,
And drink rum, rum, rum, rum,
Yo ho, yo ho, yo ho!

Leopold was standing before the tree, holding an axe.
The workmen had slowly reappeared after the dragon's
demise, and now they all stood watching as Leopold
made a very important speech.

"Progress!" he cried. "It is both our master . . . and
our slave. We enter the world with nothing, and spend
the remainder of our lives scraping and struggling
to rectify this fact. Indeed, when primitive man first
stood upright, it was not to taste the breeze, or hum

some witless ditty. It was to consume, to seek tools and possessions: the instruments of progress. And somewhere, deep in his subconscious, a voice commanded, 'Let nothing stand against you. For progress is your birthright, as a man!'"

The workmen all nodded in appreciation. They didn't quite understand what Leopold was talking about, but they all agreed that he seemed very smart and important.

"Today, we have seen hardship. Today, those who would stand against us have sought to tear asunder the very fabric of society itself! But progress is a machine far greater than any we have seen today. And progress will never be waylaid by any force or scheme. Progress is our god, gentlemen! And with this stroke, I pay tribute to its power!"

Leopold raised the axe. The tree shrank before him, and its one last leaf trembled in mortal fear.

But just as Leopold swung the axe, a little girl stepped before him in brave defense of the tree.

The blow swung wide at the very last second and landed with a smack in the mud.

"Agatha!" cried Leopold. "What is the meaning of this?"

Agatha said nothing. She simply held out the orb and offered it to her father. Leopold gazed at the golden orb and saw his own reflection. He hardly recognized himself, he thought. He looked so exceedingly mean. And yet, Leopold had progress to consider.

"I have no time for baubles!" he said, though the orb *was* most intriguing.

"It isn't a bauble," said Agatha. "It is a gift. From a friend."

Leopold didn't quite know what to do. On the one hand, he needed to chop down the tree, and build a factory, and produce more dolls, so that people would buy them and make him rich. But on the other hand, someone had given him a gift. Leopold hadn't received a gift in as long as he could remember. It was very tempting.

Perhaps he would open the gift very quickly and chop the tree down after. Yes, that was an acceptable compromise. He was already far behind schedule anyway.

So Leopold took the orb and read the inscription on its side.

To my dear friend Leopold,
with kind regards from K. Indergarten

Indergarten, Indergarten. Yes, that name rang rather a familiar bell. Leopold turned the latch, and with that the orb popped open.

Inside were a hundred tiny bugs, each bright gold in color. Even as Leopold watched, the little bugs all stood and stretched their wings. The bugs rose slowly into the air, as one, and hovered before his eyes. Leopold thought he had never seen such a beautiful thing—at least not since he had lost his imagination.

Then the bugs darted into his nose, quick as can be, and swam upward, through the tiny tunnels in his head, to his brain.

Squealing and snorting, Leopold hopped about, dancing a sort of frantic, primitive dance and clawing at his nose with both his hands.

Even Agatha didn't quite know what to make of that.

The bugs soon reached their goal. And when they did, they transformed. Some became gears, and some became cogs, and when each little bug had become a little piece of clockwork, they all came together and started to tick and to tock. Leopold Croak transformed as well, as the veil was drawn from his eyes. And as the assembled crowd looked on, Leopold experienced a vision.

Leopold stared at the tree. The tree looked sad and shy. Its one little leaf was all by itself, and soon it would surely fall, to turn brittle and brown, and be blown away by the wind. The sight made Leopold cry.

And then, pop! There was another leaf! Pop, pop, pop! There were three dozen more! As Leopold watched, one hundred million leaves came bursting forth, and the tree swelled upward, toward the sun that now shone from above.

Leopold's heart swelled with it.

From behind each and every leaf appeared a fairy with gossamer wings. The fairies sang a song, in their secret fairy tongue. The song was a message, meant just for Leopold, and only he could decipher its words. The song rose clear and high, from deep inside the fairies, and washed over Leopold like a crisp, fresh breeze in the morning. Leopold's eyes got wider and wider as he learned what he had to do.

Then the song stopped. The fairies disappeared from whence they'd come, and one hundred million leaves blew sadly away in the wind.

And the tree was just the tree once more, with its one remaining leaf. The vision had come to an end.

Leopold gasped, closed his eyes, and knew no more.

———————

Dr. Pimpledink bustled about his examining room, poking and prodding Leopold. He took the man's temperature and tested his reflexes. He massaged his two temples, and then his solar plexus. He stared down his throat. He tickled his toes. He checked Leopold's pulse, then looked up his nose. And all the while, Agatha and Miss Understood stared at Leopold with grave concern while Leopold stared back and said nothing.

Finally, after a great deal of mumbling and fumbling about, Dr. Pimpledink sat back, adjusted his spectacles, and declared Leopold fit as a fiddle and healthy as a horse.

But Miss Understood was not so sure. Miss Understood knew about such things.

"Yes," said Dr. Pimpledink knowingly. "Perhaps . . . a final test."

Dr. Pimpledink rustled around in a dusty drawer,

mumbling to himself all the while. Agatha stared at her father. He did look somehow different.

"Aha!" said Dr. Pimpledink, producing a thick stack of papers. "Now then, Mr. Croak, tell me what you see!"

On the first sheet of paper was an inkblot. Leopold stared at it for just a moment, then replied.

"A monarch butterfly, in the springtime, wearing a hat."

"And this one?"

"Siamese rhinoceri, conjoined at the horn and having a spat."

Dr. Pimpledink then presented several more in rapid succession, and much to the physician's mounting excitement, Leopold rattled them off.

"Artfully pruned bonsai sequoia. Poltergeist with paranoia. Surprisingly muscular Hindi guru. And, obviously, Cthulhu."

"And finally," whispered the doctor, "this one."

Leopold looked very closely. And when he spoke, he spoke very softly, almost as if he saw the inkblot in his mind, rather than on a piece of paper.

"It's two little pirates, climbing a tree. One . . . is Karlheinz. The other is me. I am struck down, my mind rendered lame. And Karl's heart breaks. But he wasn't to blame."

Dr. Pimpledink stood up and danced a little jig. Then he grasped Miss Understood firmly by the arm and drew her into the hall. When he spoke, he tried to be very quiet. But Agatha could both see and hear him through a small crack in the office door.

"What is your prognosis, Doctor?" asked Miss Understood, very concerned.

"But don't you see?" cried the doctor. "He's regained his imagination! And the condition is quite incurable, I'm afraid!"

Agatha ran and hugged her father just as tightly as she could. Leopold hugged her back.

It was the very first time they had hugged. And to Agatha, it felt like all the hugs she'd been missing from her father, for as long as she could remember, were suddenly given her all at once.

"You can't imagine how good it feels," whispered the girl to her father.

Leopold closed his eyes in quiet gladness, his voice cracking only slightly as he whispered softly back.

"Yes I can."

That is how Karlheinz Indergarten came to save his best and oldest friend, Leopold Croak. Karl, you see, had made for his friend a clockwork imagination, to replace the one that was lost.

But Leopold was not the only villager to regain what he had lost. No, indeed. For with his considerable fortune, Leopold worked very hard to right all the wrongs he'd caused. This had been the fairies' command, which Leopold was all too eager to obey. You see, in light of Karl's untimely absence, the children had saved the village, and Agatha the tree. So everyone had proven quite heroic in his or her own way, and now Leopold wanted to be heroic as well. He resolved to do so simply by making people happy, which is a particularly admirable brand of heroism.

The factories were thusly torn down and replaced by bakeries that made muffins.

The village pub was quickly reopened, much to the delight of certain twinkly eyed old men, who toasted Leopold's health several more times than was really necessary.

Every stray dog, and even cat, was given a home. Pim's good friend, the dog who roared like a dragon, was given a special place of honor in the home of Leopold himself, where Agatha fed him so many treats, he actually grew rather plump.

Agatha, for her part, was no longer allergic to dogs or anything else. In fact, she'd never actually been allergic to anything at all except the air, which was terribly polluted.

Soot and smog aren't good for anyone, little children most of all. The fumes that billowed from the factories had been to blame entirely. They had preyed on Agatha's immune system and played havoc with her health. But crisp, clean air soon made her better—as did a considerable dose of playtime.

And play she did. For the tree had made the most dramatic recovery of all. Leopold himself soon nursed it back to health, often comparing notes with the children on its progress. And it quickly grew one hundred million leaves, though no one was sure if there were fairies hiding behind them or not.

The tree's progress, Leopold and Agatha agreed, was far more interesting than the progress of Cuddlecom Incorporated had ever been.

So in some ways, the progress of the village moved backwards, rather than ahead, depending on how you look at it. But everyone agreed they had gone in the right direction.

There was just one way that the village really changed.

Miss Understood's Preparatory School and Home for Orphaned Children was rebuilt and, at Agatha's insistence, renamed.

They called their new school "Kindergarten."

Children liked to go there and use their imaginations.

And as Miss Understood would almost certainly say, "All's well that smells well."

CHAPTER 14

A FINAL SECRET

M adeline's grandmother stared at Madeline. Madeline stared right back.

"Well!" said the grandmother, feeling very pleased with herself. "What do you think of that?"

"I think it's the most beautiful story I've ever heard," said Madeline. "But I don't believe it."

"WHAT?" cried the grandmother. Now she was not so pleased.

"It is difficult for me to believe in beautiful things," said Madeline, "because I am a pessy-miss."

"Ah," said the grandmother. She had forgotten about that.

"I'm afraid I just can't help it," sighed Madeline.

"So it is safe to assume," said the grandmother, "that you will not be going to kindergarten."

"Oh no," said Madeline. "Certainly not."

And with that, she retreated deep into her fortress. The parley had come to a most disagreeable end.

"Very well," sighed the grandmother. "I shall inform the troops that my mission has failed."

The grandmother rose from her seat and walked very slowly to the door.

Then a head appeared from the fortress. It was Madeline.

"Grandma, whatever happened to Karlheinz?"

The grandmother paused, and though she didn't turn, she smiled a mischievous smile.

"That, my dear Madeline, is an entirely different secret altogether."

With that, the grandmother left and shut the door behind her. She walked downstairs to the kitchen, and there she announced that Madeline's case was quite hopeless, that her defenses could never be breached, and that if no one had anything else to say about the matter, she would very much like one poached egg and a muffin. Telling the story had been hard work, and it had made her hungry.

───────●

Madeline sat in her fortress and readied for sudden attack. If her parents had great catapults at their disposal, or perhaps even trebuchets, it would make for a long and tedious day of warfare.

And soon enough, sure as the world, the door to her room slowly opened.

Madeline heard someone shuffle in, and listened as the door latched shut.

Madeline peeked from the castle gates to gaze upon her enemy.

But it wasn't an enemy at all. It was her grandfather.

The grandfather sat down on the little chair by Madeline's bed and smiled.

Madeline couldn't quite help but smile back.

"I understand," said the grandfather, "that *someone* has her doubts regarding kindergarten."

"I'm afraid of it," confessed Madeline. "They'll drop me off, and I'll be all alone, without any friends or anything."

"I quite understand," said the grandfather. "It isn't easy to be without a friend."

Madeline nodded. It was true.

"So perhaps what you need . . . is a new one."

Madeline stared at her grandfather. Her grandfather stared right back. And in his eyes, Madeline thought, there was an unmistakable twinkle.

Then something moved in his shirt pocket.

Madeline didn't quite know what to make of that.

From within the shirt pocket came bounding a little clockwork mouse. It scampered down the grandfather's arm, right to Madeline's bed. And there, its whiskers twitching just slightly, it bowed.

"Pim!" cried Madeline.

The mouse, on hearing its name, turned a somersault, and proceeded to dance. And just like that, Madeline was no longer a pessy-miss, thanks to her grandfather, Mr. Karlheinz Indergarten himself.

Acknowledgments

Virtually every aspect of this book is the product of someone's imagination. Artist Dan Whisker provided the illustrations. Stuart Smith designed the book's interior. The typeface ITC Galliard, employed in the body text, was adapted by Matthew Carter, inspired by Robert Granjon's sixteenth-century design. The typeface Bembo, which graces each chapter's commencement, was created by Francesco Griffo circa 1495. Adam Kline transcribed the story, as told to him by a tiny clockwork sailor who doubtless imagined the entire affair after too many thimbles of rum.